JULES VERNE'S

20,000

LEAGUES UNDER THE SEA

RETOLD BY CARL BOWEN

ILLUSTRATED BY JOSÉ ALFONSO OCAMPO RUIZ
COLOR BY BENNY FUENTES / PROTOBUNKER STUDIO

LIBRARIAN REVIEWER
Katharine Kan
Graphic novel reviewer and Library Consultant, Panama City, FL
MLS in Library and Information Studies, University of Hawaii at Manoa, HI

READING CONSULTANT
Elizabeth Stedem
Educator/Consultant, Colorado Springs, CO
MA in Elementary Education, University of Denver, CO

STONE ARCH BOOKS
Minneapolis   San Diego

Graphic Revolve is published by Stone Arch Books,
151 Good Counsel Drive, P.O. Box 669,
Mankato, Minnesota 56002.
www.stonearchbooks.com

Library of Congress Cataloging-in-Publication Data
Bowen, Carl.
20,000 Leagues Under the Sea / by Jules Verne (retold by Carl Bowen); illustrated
José Alfonso Ocampo Ruiz.
p. cm. — (Graphic Revolve)
ISBN 978-1-4342-0447-9 (library binding)
ISBN 978-1-4342-0497-4 (paperback)
ISBN 978-1-4342-2157-5 (paperback)
1. Graphic novels. I. Ocampo Ruiz, José Alfonso. II. Verne, Jules, 1828–1905. Vingt
mille lieues sous les mers. English. III. Title.
PN6727.B683A17 2008
741.5'973—dc22   2007030804

Summary: Scientist Pierre Aronnax and his trusty servant set sail to hunt a sea monster.
With help from Ned Land, the world's greatest harpooner, the men soon discover that the
creature is really a high-tech submarine. To keep this secret from being revealed, the sub's
leader, Captain Nemo, takes the men hostage. Now, each man must decide whether to trust
Nemo or try to escape this underwater world.

Art Director: Heather Kindseth
Graphic Designer: Kay Fraser
Color by Benny Fuentes and Protobunker Studio

Printed in China

TABLE OF CONTENTS

INTRODUCING...

THE NAUTILUS

PIERRE ARONNAX
(PEE-air AHR-uh-nox)

CONSEIL
(kone-SAY)

4

CAPTAIN NEMO

NED LAND

In 1866, sailors began to notice something strange in the seas.

They sighted the mysterious creature all over the world.

At first, the strange mystery was exciting. But in 1867, the creature began to attack ships.

MONST
SIGHTED AT

TERROR ON TH
HIGH SEAS!!

According to captains
the last much off
ever fount

So, our adventure began at last.

We left from New York as heroes.

Our last reports of the narwhal put it half a world away, so we headed south.

When we reached Cape Horn, we headed north once more. This took us to the Pacific Ocean, where our hunt truly began.

9

11

Perhaps the narwhal glows in the dark.

No, wait! There it is again!

We steamed ahead at full speed, but we couldn't catch it. It stayed just out of harpoon range.

But not out of range of our cannon!

BOOOM!

We chased it away, but we couldn't sink it.

That night, when we found it again, we did not use the cannon. Instead, we relied on the king of harpooners.

When we had sailed to within 100 yards, Ned threw his weapon.

But his throw had no effect!

KLANG!

That sounded like metal!

How could that be?

13

The men took us into a dark cell inside the ship.

This is outrageous!

Stay calm, Ned.

Finally, we received a sign that our host hadn't forgotten us.

Two men came to our cell, wearing strange uniforms, and speaking a language none of us understood.

19

After that, our host offered us dinner and a tour.

Ned and Conseil wanted to eat first, but I wanted to see the ship.

Our host showed me his favorite rooms, including the engine room and his library.

Then he showed me the lounge at the front of the ship.

This ship is magnificent.

What do you call it?

The Nautilus.

Is that what the "N" on your badge stands for?

Yes, and this is the ship's motto, which means "Moving through moving waters."

MOBILIS IN N MOBILE

Goodness! I haven't even asked your name!

You may call me Nemo.

Later, I thought about the name Nemo. It's Latin, like his ship's motto. It means "No Man."

For weeks, we traveled west across the Pacific. The ship surfaced once every day to refill its air tanks and haul in nets full of food.

In my presence, the crew spoke only Nemo's secret language. Still, I could tell that they came from all over the world.

They were men like me, but they had broken all ties with the rest of the world. Could I do the same!

I didn't know.

Enjoying Hawaii, Professor Aronnax?

Is that where we are?

25

26

Enough of this!

Come inside. It's time to dive.

Nemo's words had moved me, I admit. Yet the Captain clearly hated humanity as much as he loved the sea.

What had made him this way, I could only guess. After all, he hadn't even told me his real name.

For a while after that, Nemo kept to himself, leaving us alone. We traveled day and night, on the surface and beneath the waves.

In time, we reached the Torres Strait between Australia and New Guinea.

CHAPTER 4 : Underwater Adventures

Days passed, and the support of my two dear friends comforted me.

Look! Giant jellyfish!

Are they good eating?

Better than anything that lives inside this shell, I think!

Would anyone care to join me for a walk?

Without a word, he led us to a chamber beneath the ship's propellers.

33

34

Conseil was more excited than I'd ever seen him.

Ned was tense, eager to be off the *Nautilus* for a while.

Nemo's words had put me on edge.

Only Nemo himself seemed calm about the journey that lay ahead.

I realized when I stepped out that I hadn't yet seen the whole *Nautilus*. It was more magnificent than I realized.

Nemo led us on foot into an area too delicate for the ship.

I was in heaven.

If only I could have spoken to my friends as we walked.

All the same, Nemo led us onward.

37

Eventually, we came upon a vast oyster bed. In a few months, divers would crowd this place looking for pearls.

We thought this treasure was all Nemo wanted to show us.

But it wasn't. Nemo led on.

This, it seemed, was the true object of our long walk. We were amazed.

I don't know what came over me, but I'm glad Nemo stopped me.

I could only hope he wasn't angry.

Whether he was or not, Nemo left the cave. Halfway back, the Captain turned to show us something else.

When he turned, he saw what Conseil and I saw.

Before anyone else could move, Ned threw his harpoon!

We should never have doubted the king of harpooners!

Back inside . . .

I give you my thanks, Mister Land.

Yet when your harpoon passed me, I thought you'd missed your target.

Nonsense! I never miss a target.

You might've broken all ties with humanity, but you're still a human being.

41

In no time at all, we'd reached the Mediterranean Sea!

Incredible!

We were so impressed we forgot all thoughts of escape.

We couldn't have escaped in the Mediterranean anyway.

We stayed submerged as long as we could, avoiding other ships.

We rose for air only at night.

We were traveling too fast to jump off, even in the ship's lifeboat.

45

Secretly I was glad we'd had no chance to escape. What wonders we'd have missed!

We wouldn't have seen the ruins of sunken Atlantis.

We wouldn't have seen the hidden beauty of the Sargasso Sea.

We wouldn't have sailed in upside-down valleys of Antarctic ice.

47

We traveled all the way to the South Pole itself. We were the first to locate it.

It was the only time we saw Captain Nemo set foot on dry land.

Ned just isn't suited to this life, sir.

You're right. There's nothing here for poor Ned to do.

Ah, but how things can change.

50

51

The beasts were everywhere and kept coming for so long. The more we chopped down, the more replaced them.

We saved each other's lives a dozen times that day. The beasts were too selfish to do the same for each other. They let us cut their brothers down, which we did gladly.

At day's end, they finally gave up and went back to their nests.

We lost only one man — Nemo's first mate.

Nemo thought it was his fault, but he'd done all he could.

54

We left the next morning, heading north in the *Gulf Stream*.

For weeks, we didn't see Captain Nemo. Meanwhile, Ned stayed in our cabin without speaking.

Both he and Nemo acted like men with dangerous ideas.

This worried me.

Later . . .

Sir?

Are you hurt?

Nemo! Where is Nemo?

In his cabin. He's been there for hours.

Hours! What happened with the warship?

Nemo destroyed it, sir.

It sank.

After he brought you here, he made us watch through that window!

I wish I had been struck blind first!

61

We left the *Nautilus* that morning with only the clothes on our backs.

We didn't know how far the lifeboat would take us.

But the *Nautilus* was no place for us. I finally understood that.

All I could do now was watch it disappear into the fog.

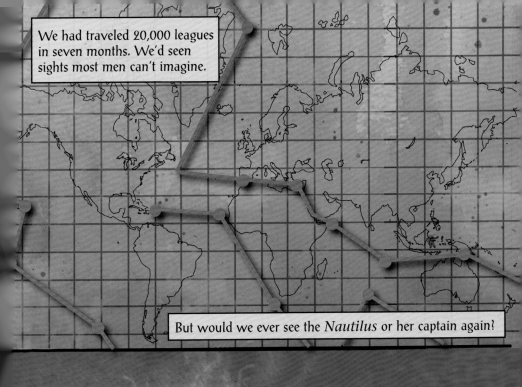

We had traveled 20,000 leagues in seven months. We'd seen sights most men can't imagine.

But would we ever see the *Nautilus* or her captain again!

I do not know.

MOBILIS IN MOBILE

ABOUT THE AUTHOR

Jules Verne was born on February 8, 1828, in France. Growing up near a river, the constant sight of ships sparked his interest in travel. As a young man, Verne even tried to run away and become a cabin boy. Fortunately, his father caught him, and soon Verne was off to study law in Paris. While there, Verne escaped the boredom of his studies by writing stories. When his father found out about this hobby, he stopped sending money for school. Verne started selling his stories, many of which became popular, including *20,000 Leagues Under the Sea* in 1870. Before he died in 1905, the author bought a boat and sailed around Europe.

ABOUT THE RETELLING AUTHOR

Carl Bowen is a writer and editor who lives in Lawrenceville, Georgia. He was born in Louisiana, lived briefly in England and was raised in Georgia where he attended grammar school, high school, and college. He has published a handful of novels and more than a dozen short stories, all while working at White Wolf Publishing as an editor and advertising copywriter. His first graphic novel, published by Udon Entertainment, is called *Exalted*. This book, *20,000 Leagues Under the Sea*, is his first book for Stone Arch Books.

GLOSSARY

binoculars (buh-NOK-yuh-lurz)—an instrument people look through to make distant objects appear closer

canal (kuh-NAL)—a passageway that connects two bodies of water

chamber (CHAYM-bur)—a small room or closed-in space

civilized (SIV-i-lized)—having manners and an education

harpoon (har-POON)—a large spear often used to hunt fish or whales

humanity (hyoo-MAN-uh-tee)—all human beings

justice (JUHSS-tiss)—a judge or someone that enforces a set of rules or laws

league (LEEG)—a unit of measurement; one **league** equals about three miles (five kilometers).

lounge (LOUNJ)—a room where people can relax, such as a living room or lobby

mobilis in mobile (MOH-bee-leess IN MOH-bee-lay)—a Latin phrase meaning "moving through moving waters"

narwhal (NAHR-wol)—a whalelike, ocean animal about 20 feet long with long tusks

theory (THEER-ee)—an idea that explains the reason for something

DIVE DEEPER
INTO SUBMARINES

Many people believe Alexander the Great was the first person to journey underwater in a contained vessel. Legend says the Greek leader explored the Aegean Sea inside a glass barrel around 333 BC, more than 2,000 years ago.

Artist Leonardo Da Vinci, who painted the famous *Mona Lisa*, also worked on plans to build an underwater ship during the 1500s. However, Da Vinci kept his plans a secret because he feared the invention would be used for war.

Less than 300 years later, Da Vinci's prediction came true. David Bushnell built the first submarine used for battle. The *Turtle*, as it was called, was made of wood, held one person, and could stay under water for a half hour. On September 6, 1776, the American army used the *Turtle* against a British warship. The attack was unsuccessful.

During the Civil War, the United States Navy tested their first submarine. The *Alligator* measured 47 feet long and could hold more than 14 crew members. While being towed into battle in 1863, a storm sunk the sub off the North Carolina coast. It has never been found.

Early subs were often powered by oars or hand-cranked propellers. The United States Navy launched the first nuclear-powered submarine in 1954. It was named the *Nautilus,* the same as Captain Nemo's underwater vessel. In 1958, the *Nautilus* became the first sub to cross beneath the North Pole.

Nuclear energy has since powered some of the fastest subs ever built, including Russia's Alfa class submarines. These subs could travel nearly 300 miles per hour!

On January 23, 1960, *Trieste* became the deepest-diving underwater vessel ever built. The *Trieste* dove nearly 38,000 feet before reaching the floor of the Pacific Ocean.

DISCUSSION QUESTIONS

1. If you were trapped in Nemo's submarine, would you want to escape like Ned Land, or would you enjoy the ride? Explain your answer.

2. Ned Land didn't seem to trust Captain Nemo. So, why do you think he saved Nemo from the shark? Explain your answer using details from the story.

3. Do you think Captain Nemo will ever get over the people he has lost and return to the surface? Or, do you think he will spend the rest of his life at sea? Why?

WRITING PROMPTS

1. Write your own underwater adventure. What would your submarine look like? Where would you travel? What type of creatures would you face?

2. At the end of the story, the *Nautilus* submarine disappears into the fog. Where do you think it will go next? Write a story about another voyage with Nemo and his crew.

3. Imagine you were going on a year-long underwater voyage and could only pack three things. What three things would you take with you and why?

OTHER BOOKS

Dracula

On a business trip to Transylvania, Jonathan Harker stays at an eerie castle owned by a man named Count Dracula. When strange things start to happen, Harker investigates and finds the count sleeping in a coffin! Harker isn't safe, and when the count escapes to London, neither are his friends.

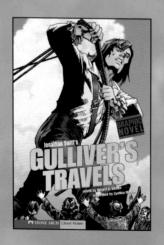

Gulliver's Travels

Lemuel Gulliver always dreamed of sailing across seas, but he never could have imagined the places his travels would take him. On the island of Lilliput, he is captured by tiny creatures no more than six inches tall. In a country of Blefuscu, he is nearly squashed by an army of giants. His adventures could be the greatest tales ever told, if he survives long enough to tell them.

Sleepy Hollow

*A headless horseman haunts Sleepy Hollow!
At least that's the legend in the tiny village of
Tarrytown. But scary stories won't stop the
town's new schoolmaster, Ichabod Crane, from
crossing through the Hollow, especially when the
beautiful Katrina Balt lives on the other side.
Will Ichabod win over his beloved or discover
that the legend of Sleepy Hollow is actually true?*

Journey to the Center of the Earth

*Axel Lidenbrock and his uncle find a mysterious
message inside a 300-year-old book. The dusty
note describes a secret passageway to the center
of the earth! Soon they are descending deeper
and deeper into the heart of a volcano. With their
guide Hans, the men discover underground rivers,
oceans, strange rock formations, and prehistoric
monsters. They also run into danger, which
threatens to trap them below the surface forever.*